T0145161

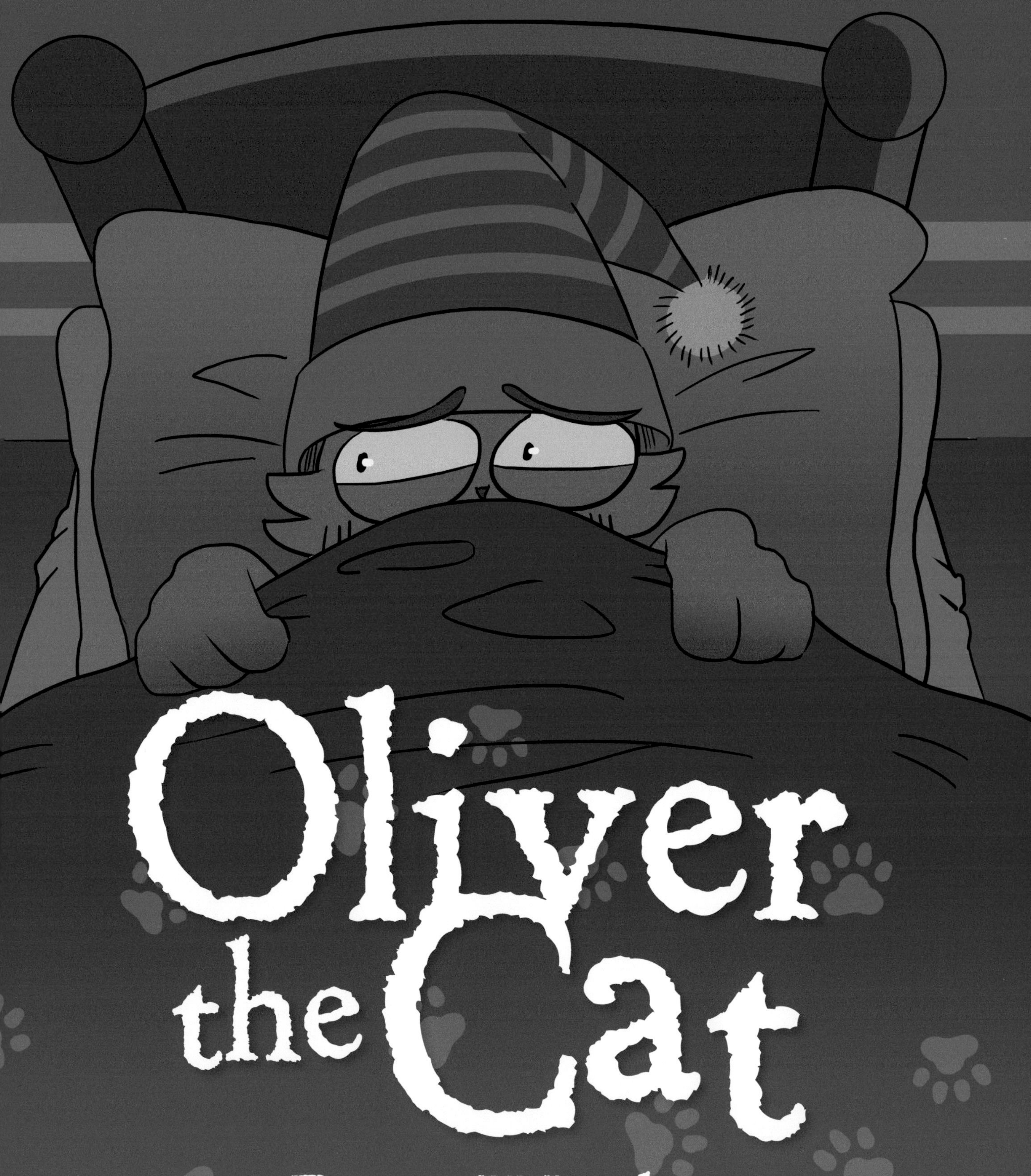

Oliver the Cat

Dawn Woods

Illustrated by: Cecil Gocotano

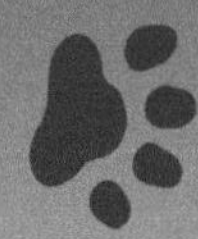

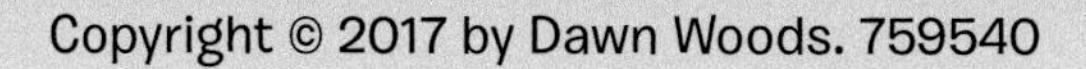

ISBN: Softcover 978-1-5434-4757-6
EBook 978-1-5434-4756-9

Print information available on the last page

Rev. date: 09/08/2017

To order additional copies of this book, contact:
Xlibris
1-888-795-4274
www.Xlibris.com
Orders@Xlibris.com

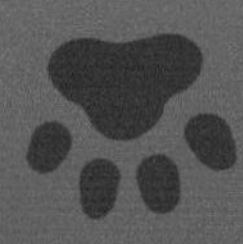

Oliver the Cat

Dawn Woods

Illustrated by: Cecil Gocotano

Meet Oliver, the striped cat,
hiding under his striped hat.

Oliver is scared of
most everything.
Things that move fast and
things that move slow,

Things that fly high
and things that fly low.

Things that make noise
or stand very still,
Things that are quiet
or let out a shrill.

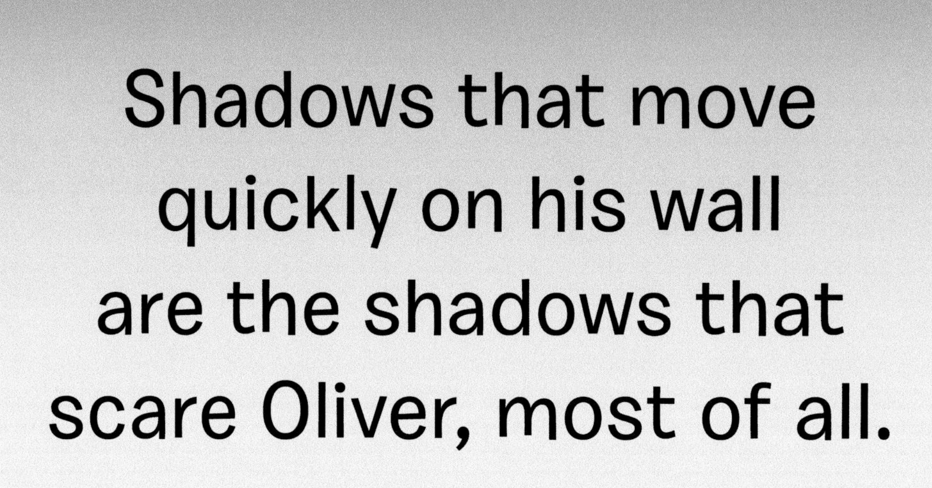

Shadows that move
quickly on his wall
are the shadows that
scare Oliver, most of all.

Noises he never EVER
hears during the day,
the noises at night
just don't go away.

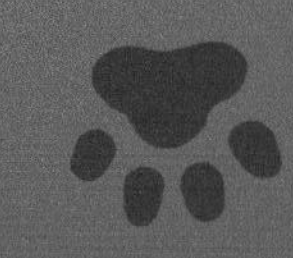

HOOT

Oh, the things he knows
that are under his bed.
He pulls down his hat
and covers his head.

Then, one night Oliver
couldn't find his hat.
He stayed wide awake
and there Oliver sat.

With his eyes wide open
and to his surprise,
all the things he “could”
see with his opened eyes.

The noises he heard
were funny too,
the forest owls were
saying, “how are you?”

HOOT!

All of the scary shadows they
seemed to disappear
Oliver, for the first time,
had nothing to fear.

Oliver now is a courageous cat
that proudly wears
his striped hat.

Printed in the United States
By Bookmasters